Magic Puppy

To Prince—such a surprise, but so sweet-natured

GROSSET & DUNLAP
Published by the Penguin Group
Penguin Group (USA) LLC, 375 Hudson Street, New York, New York 10014, USA

USA | Canada | UK | Ireland | Australia | New Zealand | India | South Africa | China

penguin.com
A Penguin Random House Company

Text copyright © 2009, 2014 Sue Bentley. Illustrations copyright © 2009 Angela Swan. Cover illustration © 2009 Andrew Farley. First printed in Great Britain in 2009 by Penguin Books Ltd. First published in the United States in 2014 by Grosset & Dunlap, a division of Penguin Young Readers Group, 345 Hudson Street, New York, New York 10014. GROSSET & DUNLAP is a trademark of Penguin Group (USA) LLC. Printed in the USA.

Library of Congress Cataloging-in-Publication Data is available.

ISBN 978-0-448-46799-3   10 9 8 7 6 5 4 3 2 1

The Perfect Secret

SUE BENTLEY

Illustrated by Angela Swan

Grosset & Dunlap
An Imprint of Penguin Group (USA) LLC

Prologue

The young silver-gray wolf bent his head to drink from the icy stream. It felt good to taste the water of his own world again.

Suddenly a fierce howl rang out in the night air.

"Shadow!" Storm gasped. The lone wolf who had attacked his Moon-claw pack was very close.

Storm should have known that it was
dangerous to come back. He needed to
find shelter, and quickly.

There was a bright gold flash and
a shower of sparks that gleamed in the
moonlight. Where the young wolf had
stood now crouched a tiny beagle puppy
with black-and-tan fur, a white muzzle,
and four white "socks" on his sturdy little
legs.

Storm hoped this disguise would
protect him until he was under cover.

His tiny puppy heart beat fast. Storm's
floppy rounded ears flew backward in the
cold wind as he leaped forward and tore
up the hillside toward a small group of
trees. The shape of a large wolf appeared
above him, outlined against the star-
bright sky.

"Here, my son. Hurry," called a deep, velvety voice.

"Mother!" Storm's tailed twirled as he dashed toward her. A wriggle began at his head and worked right down his body as he yipped a greeting.

Canista licked her disguised cub's little white muzzle. "I am pleased to see you again. You will soon be strong enough to take your place as the new leader of the Moon-claw pack. But Shadow is still looking for you."

Storm's big midnight-blue eyes gleamed with purpose. "Let us fight him now and force him to leave our lands forever." He trembled at the memory of how his father and brothers had lost their lives to the lone wolf.

Canista took a step forward, but then

bit back a cry of pain.

"You are still weak from Shadow's poisoned bite." Storm leaned forward and huffed out a puppy breath filled with a thousand tiny gold stars. The glittery mist swirled around Canista's paw for a few seconds and then sank into her thick gray fur.

"Thank you. The pain is lessening." She sighed gratefully. "But there is no time to finish the healing. You must go once more to the other world. Use this disguise and return when your magic is at its full power. I will tell the other wolves to gather and await your return."

Storm did not want to leave his mother, but he knew she was right. He nodded his tiny head.

Suddenly, another terrifying howl rang

out, sounding much closer than before. An enormous black shape appeared through the trees. The ground rang to the sound of mighty paws, which were pounding toward them.

"I know you are there, Storm. Let us finish this now!" growled a cold, pitiless voice.

"Go, Storm. Save yourself!" Canista urged.

Bright gold sparks bloomed in the tiny puppy's silky-smooth black-tan-and-white fur. Storm whined as he felt the power building in his sturdy little body. The golden glow around him grew brighter. And brighter . . .

Chapter
ONE

"Can you bring those flowers from the backseat with you, honey?" asked Madison Berry's mom.

"Okay," Madison answered with forced brightness, making a huge effort to cheer herself up. But it didn't really work. She felt as flat as a burst balloon.

Mrs. Berry let herself into the house with a spare key. "Hello! It's only us!"

"Come right in!" Madison's grandma was wearing a light blue tracksuit. She was sitting in an armchair and resting her legs on a footstool.

Madison noticed the plaster cast that covered her right foot and reached all the

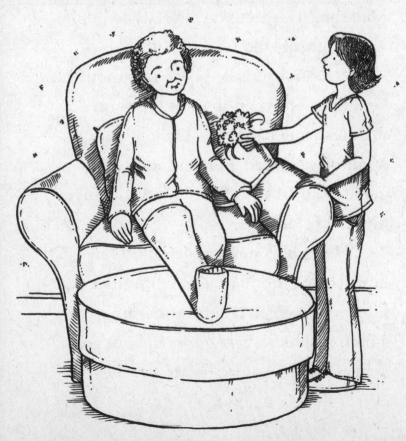

way above her knee. She went and kissed her grandma's cheek and gave her the flowers.

"Aw, thanks, honey. What beautiful pink roses! How's my favorite granddaughter?" she asked, smiling at Madison. "I expect you're pretty fed up with your silly old Grandma Jen!"

Madison had called her grandmother Grandma Jen when she was little and the nickname had stuck. Despite herself, Madison managed a smile. "Your *only* granddaughter is fine, thanks! And you're not silly or old!"

"Humph!" Grandma Jen shook her head slowly. "I don't know about that. It's not very clever to trip over the stump of a bush and break two bones in your ankle, is it? And now you've had to cancel your vacation to look after me."

"You couldn't help it. It was an accident," Madison said generously, although she'd been looking forward to the family vacation for months and months. It didn't help that her two best friends, Naomi and Shilpa, had just gone away with Naomi's parents for a whole month. Madison had gone away with Naomi last year, so this year it was Shilpa's turn.

Mrs. Berry ruffled her daughter's short dark hair approvingly. "Thanks for being so nice to your grandma," she whispered so that Grandma Jen wouldn't hear, and in a louder voice she said, "Why don't you find a vase to put those flowers in?"

Madison went into the kitchen and rooted about in the cupboards. She found a vase and filled it with water.

"It's going to be awkward for you in the shower. And you'll never get up those narrow stairs, Mom. I'm wondering if you shouldn't just come home with us." Madison could hear her mom and her grandma talking in the living room.

"Now don't worry, dear. I'll manage perfectly well down here on the recliner. And I can ask for help if I need it. It'll only be for a few weeks." Grandma Jen sighed. "I just hope I won't get too bored with all this sitting around."

"I'll come and see you," Madison promised, coming back in with the vase of flowers and placing it on the sideboard next to the fish tank. She picked up a tub of fish food. "Shall I feed the fish for you?"

Her grandma smiled broadly at her.

"Just give them a pinch. You know that I'd love you to visit, but I don't want you spending all your time looking after me. You make sure you get out and have some fun with your friends, won't you?"

Madison nodded. *I would if Shilpa and Naomi weren't about a million miles away,* she thought glumly. She wasn't looking forward to the next few weeks without them.

She sprinkled the flakes of food into the aquarium and then made her grandma some tea, while her mom organized a shopping list. Before they left, Madison fed her grandma's two birds, Sparky and Squeak, and then helped bring some bedding downstairs and make up the recliner.

"See you soon, Grandma Jen!"

Madison sang out as she closed the front door and went out to their car.

Mrs. Berry glanced across at her daughter as she drove home. "I think I'll get your grandma's groceries on the way home," she decided. "I know how you hate going grocery shopping, so why don't you stay in the car and read? It'll be quicker if I do it by myself, anyway."

"Okay. Thanks, Mom," Madison said gratefully. She had a new *Wildlife Ways* magazine in her bag. It had great pictures of colorful birds and exotic creepy-crawlies. Madison was really looking forward to reading all about them. She loved anything to do with nature—even the interesting bugs that most other kids thought were just gross.

Her mom parked under some shady

trees at the back of the parking lot and went to grab a shopping cart. Madison spread the magazine open and flipped through the pages for a while. Even with the window open, the car was broiling hot, and she decided to go and buy a cold drink.

Madison got out of the car and had only taken a couple of steps when there

was a flash of light from the flowers
planted around one of the trees. A whoosh
of golden sparks sprayed up into the air
and crackled as they hit the ground.

"Oh!" Dazzled, Madison blinked hard
and jumped sideways.

She rubbed her eyes, and when she
could see properly again, Madison noticed
that a tiny black-and-tan puppy with a
white muzzle and four white "socks" was
crawling out of the flowers. It had short
legs, large rounded floppy ears, and the
brightest midnight-blue eyes she had ever
seen.

Madison bent down and rubbed her
fingers together to encourage the cute
puppy to come closer and make friends.

"Hello. Where did you come from?"
she asked gently.

The puppy blinked its dewy eyes and put its head on one side. "I have just arrived from a place that is far from here. Can you help me?" it woofed.

Chapter
TWO

Madison snatched her hand back as if she'd been burned and looked at the puppy in complete astonishment. *No way!* She knew she had a vivid imagination, but it must be working overtime today. Dogs couldn't speak!

Suddenly, she understood. There were obviously some kids hiding nearby, playing a trick on her.

Madison straightened up and turned
around. There were bushes dotted among
the trees. She put her hands on her hips.
"Okay, you can come out now!" she
challenged. But no one emerged, and after
a few moments she looked slowly back to
where the tiny puppy was blinking up at
her.

"I don't get it," she said, puzzled.

The puppy took a few steps toward
her. It drew itself up. "I am Storm of
the Moon-claw pack. Who are you?" it
woofed.

Madison swallowed, stunned into silence. This couldn't be happening. Talking puppies didn't just appear to ordinary girls in supermarket parking lots. But this one had. Storm was looking at her quizzically, obviously expecting an answer.

"I'm M–Madison B–Berry," she found herself stammering.

Storm bowed his head. "I am honored to meet you, Madison."

"Um . . . me too. But . . . who are you? *What* are you?"

"Follow me!" Storm called, scampering past her and dashing through the trees toward a thick, spreading bush.

As Madison turned and followed the tiny puppy, there was another bright golden flash. She looked for him but he had disappeared and in his place beside the bush crouched a magnificent young silver-gray wolf with glowing midnight-blue eyes. Gold sparks glimmered like jewels in the thick ruff around its neck.

Madison gasped, eyeing the wolf's powerful muscles and sharp teeth. "Storm?"

"Yes, it is me, Madison. Do not be afraid," Storm said in a deep velvety growl.

Before Madison could get used to the incredible young wolf, there was a final dazzling flash of gold light, and Storm was once again a silky-smooth black-and-tan puppy with four little white "socks."

"Wow! That's amazing. No one would know that you're a wolf," Madison exclaimed. "But why are you in hiding?"

Storm began to tremble all over and his eyes narrowed with anger and fear. "The fierce lone wolf, who killed my father and brothers and left my mother wounded, is looking for me. He is called Shadow. Can you help me, Madison?"

"Of course I will!" Madison's heart went out to him. Storm was totally stunning as a young wolf, but as a helpless puppy, he was adorable. She bent down to pick him up and then walked back through the trees and into the parking lot.

"I'm going to ask my mom if I can keep you," she crooned, kissing the top of his soft little head and enjoying his clean puppy smell.

"Keep who? What have you got there?" asked a voice at her side.

Madison whirled around to see her mom approaching. She'd been so busy cuddling Storm that she hadn't noticed her carrying the shopping bags toward the car.

"I've just found him. Isn't he gorgeous? He's called Storm and he can ta—" Madison began, but suddenly Storm reached up and tapped her cheek with a tiny white-tipped front paw.

"Wrr–rrr–uu–ff!" he wailed loudly,
looking up at her with pleading deep-blue
eyes and shaking his head.

Madison looked down at Storm
in confusion, before it dawned on her
that Storm didn't want her to tell her
mom about his secret. She patted him
reassuringly, letting him know that she
understood, before looking back up at her
mom. "I . . . um, think Storm's a stray. Can
we take him home and look after him?"
she asked.

"Storm? You've already given him a
name? He's rather cute, isn't he? But he
was just making a strange noise as if there's
something wrong with him. The poor fella
probably needs to be taken to a vet."

"No! He doesn't. He's fine!" Madison

burst out. "I mean . . . that funny noise he made was . . . a sneeze. Um . . . because of . . . the car fumes," she said in a burst of inspiration.

Her mom looked more closely at Storm. She stroked his little head. "He certainly looks healthy enough. You might be right about the fumes. But we can't just take him home. What if he belongs to someone who's inside the store?"

Madison thought quickly. "I'll go inside and ask if anyone's reported a lost puppy."

Before her mom had a chance to protest, she ran across the parking lot. Holding Storm carefully, she went through the automatic entrance doors and hurried toward the customer-service desk.

A smart woman in a crisp blue-and-white uniform frowned at her. "I'm afraid you can't bring that puppy in here, young lady. No animals are allowed."

"Oh, sorry," Madison said, pretending that she wasn't aware of the rules. She moved slowly away from the desk and timed it so that she met her mom coming in through the automatic doors. "No one's reported a lost puppy," she said, taking her mom's arm and gently steering her back out. *It wasn't exactly a fib*, she thought, *since I didn't even ask about one*. "So can we look after Storm? I'll do everything for him: take him for walks, feed him, wipe up muddy paw prints, bathe him . . ."

Her mom sighed. "It's not really a good time. We've got your grandma to look after, and I for one don't look forward to the complications of puppy accidents and chewed slippers."

Storm gave an indignant little woof at the very idea that he might not be fully housebroken.

Madison had to try hard not to grin. She forced herself to look serious again.

"Oh, please, Mom. Please, please," she begged. "Look how cute he is. He'll take up hardly any room. And Grandma Jen will love Storm. You know how she is about animals. And she's really sad about her ankle, and she can't go out much. I bet it'll cheer her up to have a puppy to cuddle," she rushed on.

"Enough already!" Her mom held up her hands. "I suppose we could give it a try. But I don't know what your dad's going to say when he sees him."

"He'll love him to pieces, like I do!"

Mrs. Berry smiled. "You're probably right at that. You do realize that I'm going to have to report Storm as a stray? If someone comes forward to claim him, there'll be no arguments. Okay?"

"It's a deal!" Madison agreed readily,

positive that no one was going to come calling for her new little friend. Before she'd met Storm she'd been feeling really down in the dumps about her family's canceled vacation and having no friends to hang out with. But the long, lonely weeks ahead were starting to look a bit brighter already.

Chapter
THREE

"You must be hungry after your long journey," Madison said, forking some leftover casserole into a bowl. It was the closest thing she had to dog food, so it would have to do.

Storm licked his lips eagerly. The moment she put the bowl onto the kitchen floor, he bounded forward and began chomping the food.

Madison watched him, smiling. It was still hard to believe that this magic puppy had chosen her to be his friend.

Storm finished eating and sat licking his chops, while Madison washed his dish and put it away.

"He polished that off pretty quickly!" Madison's mom said from over by the kitchen counter where she was making supper.

"I'll take him upstairs to show him where he'll be sleeping," Madison said

happily. "Come on, Storm. Let's go!" she called.

Storm immediately jumped to his feet and scampered across the kitchen toward her.

Mrs. Berry watched them. "That puppy seems to know exactly what you're saying," she commented.

Madison smiled to herself. If only her mom knew!

"I'm sorry that I almost gave away your secret to Mom earlier," she whispered to Storm as they climbed the stairs.

"I do not think she noticed. Grown-up humans seem to find it hard to believe in magic," he woofed. His furry brow creased as he looked serious. "But you must never tell anyone my secret. Promise me, Madison."

"Oh," Madison said, disappointed. She

had been hoping that she could share her wonderful news with Grandma Jen, who was great at keeping secrets. But she was prepared to do anything to help keep the tiny puppy safe. "Okay then. Cross my heart. I won't say anything to anyone. You're safe with me."

Storm looked up at her, his deep-blue eyes shining. "Thank you, Madison."

In her bedroom, Madison spread a piece of old blanket on top of her comforter. She patted it encouragingly. "Mom says you have to sleep on this because she doesn't want puppy hairs all over the bed. But I don't mind them. You can sleep next to me when we're by ourselves."

Storm sprang up onto the bed, leaving a shower of faint gold sparks in the air behind him.

"Wow! Isn't that a dead giveaway?"
Madison asked, eyeing the glittery trail.
"I mean—someone's going to notice if
little sparks fly off you all the time, aren't
they?"

"I will use my magic, so that only
you can see and hear me completely," the
puppy woofed. "Other humans will think
I am an ordinary puppy."

"You can do that? Cool! That makes
things much easier," Madison said
delightedly.

Storm sniffed at the blanket and
then scrabbled it into messy folds, before
turning around and lying down. "This is
a safe place!" he sighed contentedly.

Madison sat down beside him. "I'm
glad you like it, because I love having
you living with me."

She stroked the little pup as she
stared idly out of her bedroom window.
It overlooked a large area of overgrown
land, which reached down to the river.
A huge factory used to stand on the
site, but it had been torn down years
ago.

Clumps of waist-high nettles and
brambles covered with starry-white
flowers sprawled everywhere. Bushes
and tall weeds had sprouted up around
the trees, turning the field into a mini
jungle.

Storm sat up and craned his neck to

look for movements in the long grass, and Madison saw his eyes gleam and his floppy ears twitch with sudden interest.

"Rabbits!" he yapped.

"Yes. I sometimes borrow Dad's binoculars to watch them. There are lots of birds and butterflies, too, and I even saw a fox once. There's a gap in the fence that no one's bothered to fix, and lots of people take their dogs for walks there. Would you like to check it out?"

Storm leaped to his feet again, his whole body quivering with eagerness. "Walking is my favorite thing!"

Madison smiled. "Come on, then. I'll just go and tell Mom where we're going. We can't be long, because Dad will be home soon and we'll be having dinner."

Madison went outside with Storm at her heels. They were walking the few feet to the gap in the fence when a dark green jeep drew up. A fair-haired man wearing a camouflage jacket, walking boots, and pants with lots of pockets got out and opened the trunk.

He nodded and smiled at Madison
and Storm. "Hello there, young lady. Cute
puppy!" he said, unloading a knapsack and
a camera.

Madison smiled back at him, before he
went into the field.

She noticed that there were lots
of colorful stickers with badgers, birds,
and insects on them stuck to the jeep's
bumper. *He must be really interested in
wildlife,* she thought.

Madison stepped through the gap
in the fence and Storm followed her.
He gave an eager little woof and dived
beneath a tangle of grass and leaves. As he
weaved around, trying to sniff out rabbit
trails, Madison could just see the white tip
of his cute little tail poking into the air. At
one point he disturbed a wood pigeon.

It rose up from a bush with a noisy flutter of wings.

"Yikes!" Storm skipped sideways with his tail between his legs.

Madison grinned at his antics. She walked on, leaving him to explore and run off some energy. They didn't see the man from the jeep again, and Madison assumed that he was bird-watching.

Time was getting on and she decided to double back and head for home.

"Storm! Come here, boy! Let's go!"

Storm came hurtling toward her with his tongue hanging out and his floppy ears flying out behind him. There were greenish streaks of something nasty all over him. As he reached her she got a pungent whiff.

"Yuck! You smell terrible," she groaned.

"Mom will go crazy when she sees you. I'm going to have to smuggle you up to the bathroom."

Storm's small white teeth flashed in a doggy grin. "I like the interesting smells on my fur. But I will roll in the grass to get myself clean!" he woofed.

Madison couldn't help laughing. "Trust me. That's *not* going to work."

Chapter
FOUR

Mr. Berry was in the hall when
Madison and Storm came downstairs
together. Madison's dad had changed out of
his work suit into jeans and a polo shirt.

"Hi, Madison. Hello, little fella! I just
heard all about you," he said, bending
down to scratch Storm under the chin. "It's
going to be nice to have a puppy around
the house."

Madison was relieved that her dad hadn't made a big deal about her new friend. Her mom must have filled him in about all the details. Storm wagged his tail and he licked Mr. Berry's fingers, enjoying all the fuss.

"What's that smell? Have you been using that expensive shower gel I bought for your mom's birthday, Madison?" her dad said suspiciously, looking up at her.

"What, me? No way," Madison said innocently. *But Storm has!*

"Supper's on the table!" her mom called from the kitchen, which saved Madison from answering more questions.

"Great! I'm starving." Madison quickly scooped up Storm and shot into the kitchen with him. She put the puppy down and he curled up sleepily under the

table, with his head resting on her feet.

Madison heaped food onto her plate. As they ate, she told her mom and dad about the man in the jeep. "He seemed to have a lot of camera equipment."

Mrs. Berry looked interested. "Perhaps someone's finally going to do something about that land. It's a terrible eyesore. It's so overgrown, and there are always letters in the local paper about kids hanging around the property and causing trouble. I'd rather some nice new houses were built there."

"I like it how it is. It's good for wildlife," Madison said.

"Animals always come first with you, don't they?" her dad said, smiling. "You're just like your grandma. She spent a fortune on that fancy birdcage for Sparky and Squeak, and I've lost count of the number of bird feeders in her garden." He turned to his wife. "How was Mom today? Is she coping with that cast on her leg?"

Madison's mom told him all about their visit earlier. "Her only worry is that she'll get bored. Madison and I will drop by to see her tomorrow and take her shopping."

"Aren't you forgetting someone?" Madison asked. "Storm! Grandma Jen will be so surprised when she sees that I've got a new puppy."

Her mom and dad laughed. "I expect she will," her dad agreed.

After they finished eating, Madison helped clear away the dishes and went into the living room with Storm. "There's a great show about deep-sea creatures just starting," she told him.

"Sounds good. I'll watch it with you," her dad said.

Madison realized that she had spoken louder than she'd meant to. She'd have to be more careful about keeping Storm's secret.

Madison sat on the sofa next to her dad and settled Storm on her lap. He seemed fascinated by the weird-looking fishes with huge eyes and long curved teeth that loomed out of the inky darkness of the ocean depths.

"Aren't they amazing?" Madison said.
"Like creatures from another planet!"

"I must say that you're very cheerful
for someone who's just had their vacation
canceled and who was saying how much she
was missing her two best friends," her dad
commented.

A pang of guilt rose up inside Madison.
She'd hardly thought about Shilpa and Naomi

over the last few hours. She wasn't
missing them nearly as much now that
she had a new furry friend. She shrugged,
stroking Storm's silky ears. "There's no
use stressing out over stuff you can't
change, is there?" she said thoughtfully.

After the TV show was over, Madison
took Storm upstairs, planning to relax
with him and finish reading her wildlife
magazine. But Storm seemed to have
other ideas. He scampered across the
room and leaped onto a chair near
the window. He stood up on his short
back legs and put his front paws on the
windowsill.

"What are you looking at?" Madison
asked, going over to stand beside him.
"The place down there that was full of
exciting smells," he woofed, looking up at

her hopefully with big eyes and wagging his tail.

"I'll take you over there again tomorrow morning," she promised. "Oh, look. There's that man we saw earlier."

The fair-haired man in the camouflage jacket was stepping through the gap in the fence.

"He's been over there for hours," Madison said, hoping as hard as she could that he didn't have anything to do with the houses that her mom had said might be built on the land. Madison stroked Storm's silky ears as they watched him load his equipment in the jeep, before driving away.

Chapter
FIVE

The following morning, Madison
woke up bright and early to find sunshine
pouring through a crack in the curtains.
There was a warm weight on one arm.
She smiled and reached out to stroke
Storm, who was cuddled up close to her.

"Did you sleep well?" she asked him.

"Very well, thank you," Storm woofed
politely. He stood up and gave himself a

shake. "I am ready for a walk now!"

Smiling at his eagerness, Madison jumped out of bed and threw on some jeans, a T-shirt, and sneakers. She could hear movements in the bathroom as her dad got ready for work.

She fed Storm in the kitchen and was hastily cramming toast into her mouth

when her dad came in.

"Slow down, Madison! Where's the fire?" he teased.

"Storm said that he wants to—" Madison stopped. "I mean, I want to take Storm for a walk in the field before Mom and I go to Grandma Jen's," she quickly corrected.

Luckily, her dad was searching his pockets for his car keys and didn't notice.

"Have a good day at work! Later!" she called out as she rushed out of the kitchen and headed toward the front door, with Storm running after her.

As they walked down the street, Madison noticed that the green jeep was parked there again. There was no sign of the man, so she assumed he must be bird-watching in the field.

Madison noticed a girl, who looked

about twelve years old, coming down the street toward them. She had a friendly face and her blonde hair was tied back in a ponytail.

"Hi!" the girl said, pausing as she drew level. "Do you live around here? I wondered if you knew where the nearest convenience store is."

"I live just up the road. There's a store just around the corner," Madison said helpfully. "It sells sandwiches and stuff."

"Oh, right. Thanks. I'm Ellie Robertson, by the way," the girl said.

"Hi, Ellie. I'm Madison."

Ellie smiled. "Your puppy's gorgeous. What's his name?"

"Storm," Madison told her.

Storm wagged his tail and looked up at Ellie.

The older girl bent down to stroke the tiny puppy. "I love dogs. Storm doesn't look very old. Have you had him long? I don't think I've ever seen a puppy with such amazing big blue eyes."

"Me, neither. Storm's one of a kind. I just got him," Madison said fondly. "I haven't

seen you around here before," she said, changing the subject before Ellie asked any awkward questions.

"I'm here with my dad. He's a naturalist. That's our car," Ellie said, pointing toward the jeep. "I'm helping Dad right now since I'm on school break. He never thinks of food when he's working, but he'll want lunch later and expect me to produce something by magic!"

Madison knew that a naturalist was someone who studies animals and plants. It was something she'd love to do when she grew up. "Are you looking at birds? We get lots in the field."

Ellie shook her head. "Dad's special interest is small mammals. He thinks there could be field mice nearby."

"Oh wow!" Madison said excitedly.

"Field mice aren't usually found in this area, are they? They're so cute with those dark coats, pink noses, and big round bodies."

"Yeah, they are rare around here," Ellie said, looking surprised. "You seem to know all about them."

"I don't really," Madison admitted. "I've seen pictures and read a bit about them. I'd love to get a close look at a real one." She remembered something else she'd read. "They are also called meadow voles, aren't they?"

Ellie nodded. "That's right. But Dad and I have always called them field mice—we think the name suits them better. Why don't you come over and see how we're doing later? Dad won't mind."

"I'd love to!" Madison said.

"Okay then. I'd better get those

sandwiches. Bye! Bye, Storm," Ellie said,
giving him a gentle pat.

Madison waved as Ellie walked away.
"She seemed really nice, didn't she?"

Storm nodded. "I liked her, too."

Madison and Storm continued on
their way to the field. They were almost
there when three boys, holding cans
of soda, burst through the gap in the
fence. Madison recognized them from

school. They were two years older than her
and were always getting into trouble and
picking on smaller kids.

She felt herself tensing as the boys
scrunched up the cans and began kicking
them around. Laughing and jostling each
other, they kicked a can in her direction.

It bounced very close to Storm. He
yapped in surprise and had to skip sideways
to avoid being struck.

"Hey, watch out!" Madison cried
protectively.

One of the boys frowned. He was small
and stocky, and there was a mean look on
his face. "Who do you think you are, telling
us what to do?" he challenged.

Madison took a step backward as the
tough boy nudged his friends. They spread
out across the path, barring her way.

"Excuse me. I . . . I want to get to the field," she said, her heart thumping.

"Tough! You'll have to go around the block, won't you?" the stocky boy sneered.

Madison gulped, wondering whether to risk walking toward the three of them in the hope that they'd let her through. But the boys folded their arms and stood their ground.

Storm growled softly. Madison felt a peculiar warm tingling sensation flow down her spine as large gold sparks ignited in Storm's smooth fur and his broad floppy ears crackled and fizzed with miniature lightning bolts.

Something very strange was about to happen.

Chapter
SIX

Madison watched in complete amazement as Storm raised a white-tipped front paw and a shower of sparks whooshed out and turned into a cloud of tiny flies. They whirled around the boys, buzzing annoyingly, getting into their hair, and crawling on their skin.

"Argh!" the boys yelled, batting their hands and hopping about.

"Where did they come from?"

"Yuck! I just swallowed one!" the stocky boy complained.

"I think I've got one in my pants!" yelled his friend, jumping up and down.

Madison started laughing as the boys tore down the street pursued by the cloud of itchy flies and disappeared around the corner. "You are so bad, Storm! But it served those bullies right!"

Storm grinned mischievously as every last golden spark faded from his fur. "I am glad that I could help!"

Madison stepped into the field and
Storm followed her. They took one of the
narrow pathways that wove through the
long grass. "Don't get all muddy again,"
she warned him. "We're going straight
over to my grandma's house when we get
back, and I don't have time to give you
another bath."

At the word *bath*, Storm wrinkled his
nose. He was careful to avoid any ditches
and instead, rooted out a mossy old stick.
Madison grinned as he ambled along with
it proudly grasped in his mouth.

Madison spotted Ellie and her dad
with a camera and tripod near a patch
of brambles in the distance. Ellie saw her
looking and waved.

Madison was really tempted to jog

over and see what they were doing, but she decided that she'd better go home. Her mom would be impatient to leave, and Grandma Jen was expecting them.

She looked down at Storm. "We can come back again tomorrow. I'd love it if Ellie's dad found field mice."

* * *

"Goodness me!" Grandma Jen exclaimed delightedly, the moment Madison walked in with Storm in her arms. "You didn't say anything about having a new puppy when you left yesterday! Where did he come from?"

You wouldn't believe me if I told you, Madison thought.

She put Storm on the recliner and then explained about finding him in the supermarket parking lot. "I knew you'd like him. I already love Storm so much."

"I can see why. He's irresistible." Grandma Jen's eyes softened as Storm stepped carefully onto her lap and curled into a ball. She stroked his silky-smooth fur. "A dog's such a wonderful companion," she said quietly.

Madison thought her grandma sounded rather sad. It had been a long

time since Grandpa had died. She knew
that despite their regular family visits,
Grandma Jen sometimes got lonely,
although she didn't like to admit it.
Madison had a sudden idea. "I know! Why
don't *you* get a puppy?" she said eagerly.

Storm wagged his tail and gave a woof
of agreement.

"Me?" Grandma Jen said, frowning. "I
wouldn't know where to start looking for
one!"

"That's easy-peasy," Madison said.
"Lots of dogs need homes. You just phone
up the animal shelter—"

"Now Madison, don't get carried
away," Mrs. Berry warned as she came in
from the kitchen with a sandwich and a
drink on a tray. "Your grandma's ankle's
going to take at least two months to heal.

The last thing she wants is an energetic
new puppy."

"But I could help her train it and
take it for walks with Storm. And it
would cheer her up and . . ." As her mom
raised her eyebrows, Madison trailed off.
"Okay—bad idea." She sighed.

Grandma Jen winked at Madison and
reached out to squeeze her hand. There
was a rebellious spark in her eye. "I'll
think about what you said," she said softly.
"Anyway, what have you been doing, apart
from having fun with Storm?"

"Well—we just met a really nice girl
named Ellie. She's helping her dad look
for field mice in the field next to our
house," Madison explained.

"Field mice? I used to see those quite
a lot when I was a girl." Grandma Jen said.

"We had a swampy area at the back of our cottage. It's hard to imagine that the little creatures would be around here."

"Yes, it's really strange. But wouldn't it be cool if there *are* field mice in our field? That would make it a really special place," Madison enthused.

"Well, I'm not crazy about having a bunch of mice running around," Mrs. Berry said, shuddering. "They might infest

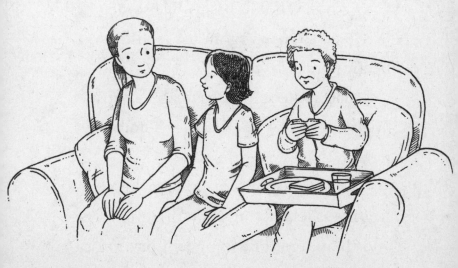

our house when their food starts running out in the winter."

"Mo-om! They wouldn't. They're not that sort of mouse," Madison protested. "And, anyway, field mice eat grasses and plants, so they don't need any of our food."

"Quite right," her grandma agreed. "And I don't know why's there's so much fuss in the papers about that field being an eyesore. Wildlife has to live somewhere. We need to make room for it in this hectic world."

Madison couldn't have agreed more. She felt a stir of affection for Grandma Jen.

While her grandma ate her lunch, Madison helped put away the groceries and then hung out some laundry to dry in the garden. Soon afterward, they said their good-byes and left, but not before Grandma Jen insisted on giving Storm a final cuddle.

"You come and see me again, very soon," she said to him.

Storm woofed softly in answer, and licked the end of her nose with his little pink tongue.

Chapter
SEVEN

Saturday dawned bright and clear.
The moment breakfast was over, Madison
dashed out of the house, with Storm
scampering after her, and headed for
the field. "I wonder how Ellie and her
dad are doing. I can't wait to see my
first ever real, live field mouse!" she said
enthusiastically.

"I would like to see one, too. I do not

think we have them in my home world,"
Storm yapped.

Madison tried to imagine what a
wintry world ruled by magnificent wolves
would be like. She thought of sunlight
glinting on a vast frozen landscape of
mountains, lakes, and forests. It must be
cold and beautiful and very dangerous.

"Uh-oh." Madison spotted the three
tough boys at the end of her street. They
all held sticks and were running them
along some railings to make a clattering
noise. Luckily, the boys disappeared around
the corner without seeing them.

Madison and Storm quickly slipped
through the fence and went looking for
Ellie and her dad. Storm snuffled along,
head down and tail up. They rounded a
huge, tangled clump of brambles and came

upon Ellie writing in a notebook.

"Hi! How's it going?" Madison asked.

Ellie looked up and smiled. "Hi! We've made some progress. Come and have a look." She led the way to where her dad had set up his camera and tripod. His canvas bag was open on the ground. "Dad, this is Madison, who I told you about.

You met her the other day."

Mr. Robertson smiled. "Hello, Madison. I remember. And this must be Storm."

Storm blinked up at him and wagged his tail. *Grr-uf!*

"Hello, Mr. Robertson," Madison said politely.

"Call me Oliver. Everyone does."

"Can we show Madison what we've found?" Ellie asked, reaching into his bag and taking out a small cardboard box.

Madison bent close as Ellie opened the flap. Inside the box was a rather messy and loosely woven nest, made of stripped stems, grass, and bramble leaves. "Was there anything inside?" she asked hopefully.

Oliver shook his head. "We found this on the ground, next to a burrowed tunnel.

It's quite fresh, so it's probably in use.
Unfortunately, there were some kids over
here earlier, messing around and swiping at
the grass with sticks."

"Dad asked them to be careful, but they
just talked back," Ellie put in, obviously
upset.

Madison didn't need three guesses to
know who the boys were. "So . . . are there

any babies?" she asked worriedly.

"They're probably safe. The female field mouse is very protective, so she would take care of them."

"Oh, good," Madison said, relieved.

Storm reared up and poked his head forward to look into the box. He sniffed at it, his tail wagging interestedly.

"Getting the scent are you, little fella?" Oliver smiled and stroked the tiny puppy's floppy ears. He turned back to Madison. "At least we're pretty sure now that field mice are around. But we need to find more nests before we can be certain."

"We're going to do a night watch tomorrow," Ellie told her. "At this time of year, field mice are more active at night, and we've got a better chance of seeing them."

"Can we come and help?" Madison asked eagerly.

Oliver smiled. "Any extra help's always welcome. But I'm not sure that it's a good idea to bring Storm. If he starts barking and getting overexcited, he'll ruin our chances of seeing any field mice."

"Storm would never do that. He's very well trained," Madison assured him, but she could see that Oliver still looked doubtful. "I'll show you," she said on impulse. "Sit!" she ordered, hoping Storm got the message.

Storm blinked at her in surprise, but obediently sat down.

"Good boy. Now, stay," Madison said firmly. She turned her back and walked about twelve feet away, keeping her fingers crossed.

Storm didn't run after her. He stayed put, as if waiting for another command.

Madison turned around and walked back toward him. She stopped in front of him and lifted her hand. To her amazement Storm stood up, wove neatly around her legs and sat down at heel with his tail tucked beneath him.

"Wow! You two are great. How many hours at puppy-training classes did that take?" asked Ellie.

"Oh . . . um, not as many you might think," Madison said vaguely.

"I guess we'll see you *and* Storm, tomorrow night then," Oliver said.

"You bet!" Madison said, grinning as she moved away. "That was impressive," she whispered to Storm when they were out of earshot. "How did you know what to do?"

Storm put his head on one side as he looked at her. "I have seen pet dogs act like that with their humans. I just copied them!"

Madison planned to walk over and visit her grandmother the following afternoon. The phone rang just as they were about to set off. It was Grandma Jen.

"I'm glad I caught you. I wondered if you'd mind dropping by the pet store for me?" she asked. "I've almost run out of birdseed."

"No problem," Madison told her.

She loved the pet store with its warm, musty smell, tanks of tropical fish, and cages full of small birds, hamsters, and gerbils. Madison and Storm spent some time looking around, before buying seed for Sparky and Squeak and a soft ball and some chew toys for Storm.

At her grandma's house, Madison fed the birds and then suggested they all go out into the garden so Storm could play with his new ball. Grandma Jen hobbled outside with her walker and sat in a garden chair.

Storm enjoyed a lively game of

fetch. Grandma Jen and Madison took turns throwing the ball for him, and he raced around after it with his pink tongue hanging out. Afterward he flopped onto the lawn, panting.

Grandma Jen enjoyed the playful pup's antics. "You two are better than medicine!

You really cheer me up." She looked
quizzically at Madison. "Did you mean
it about helping me to look after a new
puppy and taking it for walks?"

Madison did a double take.
"Definitely! So—does that mean you're
getting one? When is it—"

"Calm down, honey. Nothing's
decided yet," her grandma interrupted
kindly.

Madison sighed. Why did grown-ups
always take so long making their minds up
about things?

"Shall I water your veggies for you?"
she said, turning on the outside tap and
hauling the hose across the lawn.

As a stream of water splashed out,
Storm made an amazing recovery and
jumped to his feet. Bouncing down onto

his front legs, he waggled his tiny rear end.
He pounced on the hose, barking and
snapping at the stream of water.

"You're a clown!" Madison whispered
affectionately so that Grandma Jen couldn't
hear. "I hope you can stay with me forever
and ever."

A serious expression crossed Storm's
little face. He sat down and looked up at
her. "I cannot do that. One day I must
return to my homeland and the Moon-claw
pack. Do you understand that, Madison?"

"Um . . . yes. But that won't be for a
long time, will it?" she asked hopefully.

"I do not know," Storm admitted. "But
if Shadow finds me, I may have to leave
suddenly, without saying good-bye."

Madison felt a sharp pang, as she knew
that she'd never be ready to lose her furry

friend. She pushed the uncomfortable idea
to the back of her mind and made a firm
promise with herself to enjoy every single
moment with Storm.

Chapter
EIGHT

As the sun went down, the evening sky was painted in glorious shades of orange, pink, and violet. Madison glanced out of the kitchen window, watching as the first stars appeared.

"I'm not sure it's a good idea for you to go crawling around that field in the dark all by yourself," Madison's mom said doubtfully as she finished unloading the dishwasher.

"But I'll be with Storm!" Madison protested. "And Ellie and her dad will be there. I'll be fine!"

"I think your mom's right," her dad said, coming into the kitchen. "It's too dangerous. You could easily stumble into a ditch and hurt yourself. I'll come with you. I'll just go and change my shoes."

"Oh great!" Madison complained to Storm as her mom and dad both went into the hall. "They still think I'm about four instead of nearly nine years old."

Storm's ears twitched and he gave a shrill whine and began pawing frantically at the back door. Madison opened it for him automatically, still feeling grumpy about having to bring her dad along like a little kid.

It was a moment before she realized

that a loud snapping and growling noise
was coming from outside the front of the
house.

She ran into the sitting room and
peered out of the window. A man
struggling with two large dogs on leashes
was walking beneath a streetlight. Madison
saw that the dogs seemed to have pale,
wolf-like eyes and extra-large teeth. They
were straining to get into the front yard.

The man managed to get them under control and shut them in the backseat of a nearby car before driving off.

Madison shivered. Those dogs gave her a very bad feeling.

A horrible suspicion crept over her as she remembered what Storm had said to her at Grandma Jen's earlier about having to leave suddenly if Shadow found him.

Shadow had sent those dogs!

Somehow, Madison knew that she was right. Storm must have heard them growling at the front of the house and rushed outside to hide. Her heart was in her throat as she ran into the backyard.

"Storm! Where are you?" she whispered. "You're safe. You can come out now!"

But however much Madison called, he

didn't answer. A guilty feeling rose in her chest. Why hadn't she paid more attention when he'd pawed at the back door?

What if Storm had gone? It was unbearable to think that she would never see her puppy friend again.

After carefully checking the back garden and finding no sign of Storm, Madison raced around the side of the house. She emerged into the street just in time to catch sight of a small dark shape speeding headlong toward the gap in the fence. Four little white "socks" gleamed in moonlight.

Madison's heart leaped with relief. "Storm!"

She shot after the terrified puppy without a second thought. Reaching the fence, she stumbled through the gap. Too

far away now from street lights, she stood
blinking, her eyes trying to adjust to the
sudden darkness. She could barely see a
foot in front of her, but there was no time
to run back home for a flashlight.

"Storm! It's me. Where are you?" she
called.

Twigs snapped under her feet and there
were rustling noises in the nearby bushes
as Madison pushed ahead. She narrowly
avoided running into a tree. Lurching to
one side, she almost went sprawling as her
foot disappeared down a hole.

"Ow!" Thrown off balance, she fell
sideways, wrenching her leg. Pain shot
through her knee, making her gasp, but she
ignored it and limped forward.

Branches tugged at Madison's hair and
brushed against her face as she pressed on

blindly. Brambles and tall thistles loomed
out from the darkness. The familiar field
now seemed strange and menacing.

Madison stopped, panting. Even the
faint light from the gap in the fence had
disappeared, and she couldn't tell which
direction she was facing.

"Storm!" she whispered desperately.
"Shadow's dogs have gone. You're safe now.
Please, come out!"

Madison heard a faint whimper and
a tingling feeling crept down her spine. A
tiny light appeared, which grew brighter as
Storm crawled out from behind an old log
and came toward her. His whole body was
glowing softly like a lantern and spreading
golden light in a three-feet-wide circle.

"Oh, thank goodness!" Madison
breathed as she swept him up and wrapped

her arms around him. She could feel his
tiny heart beating against her palms. "I'm
really sorry. I was so busy thinking about
myself back there that I didn't realize
you were in danger," she apologized,
swallowing guilty tears.

Storm licked her chin with his warm
tongue.

"It does not matter. You came here by
yourself to find me. You were very brave."

"I wasn't, really. I'm just glad you're all

right. I couldn't bear to see anything to happen to you. Oh!" Madison gasped as a fresh wave of pain stabbed at her knee. Now that she had found Storm, she felt sick and her legs had gone all wobbly.

"You are hurt, Madison. I will make you better."

Storm huffed out a warm breath that glinted with a thousand tiny gold stars. The sparkly mist swirled around Madison's knee for a few seconds before it sank into her jeans and disappeared. The pain grew hot and sharp for a moment, but then began to ebb away just as if it had gone out with the tide at the seashore.

"Thanks, Storm. I'm fine now," she whispered gratefully, reaching out to pick him up. "Maybe we'd better go back home and get a flashlight. I don't know whether

Ellie and Oliver are here yet. I wasn't exactly looking for their jeep when I ran after you. Oh heck—Dad!" she gasped, remembering that he was supposed to be coming with her and would probably be wondering where she'd gone.

She was about to ask Storm to help her find the way back through the darkness, when a bloodcurdling cry rang out. Twigs snapped and branches cracked as two shadowy fingers leaped out of the bushes. There was thud as a third figure jumped down from a tree.

A hand grabbed her arm. "Don't move!" a rough voice ordered.

Chapter
NINE

Madison cried out in alarm. She clutched Storm against her. Was this another of Shadow's attacks? Her pulse raced at the thought of facing Storm's fierce enemy.

"This is our hideout, and you're trespassing!" another voice yelled.

Flashlight beams lit up three familiar faces streaked with brown and green paint beneath green camouflage bandanas. It was the three older boys from Madison's school.

Relief swept through Madison. Her fear faded and suddenly she was angrier than she had ever been in her life.

"You stupid, stupid idiots!" she raged. "Why don't you guys act your age? I almost had a heart attack!"

"Who are you calling an idiot?" asked the small stocky boy, who seemed to be the ringleader.

"What are we going to do with her, Sam?" another boy asked.

"Take her prisoner," Sam said. "And grab that goofy-looking puppy she's holding. We'll tie it to that log."

"I wouldn't try that, if I were you!" Madison warned.

"Yeah! Are you gonna stop me?"

Storm's lip curled as he showed his teeth to the boys. "Put me down, Madison," he growled softly.

Madison quickly yanked her arm free, bent down, and did as he asked. Storm vanished instantly into the shadows.

"Hey! Where did that mangy mutt go?" one of the boys said.

"Forget it. Grab her!" Sam ordered.

Madison folded her arms and calmly faced the three boys. They paused in

surprise, obviously expecting her to
try and run. She felt a strong prickling
sensation down her spine and heard a faint
crackling of magical sparks from one of
the bushes.

"One, two . . . three," she counted.

Whoosh! A mini tornado of grass
and leaves rose into the air. It whirled
toward the boys, forging a path through
the weedy grass. *Swirl!* It knocked them
off their feet. Three stunned faces gazed
at Madison as they whizzed around and
around in a dizzy twirl as if they were in
a dryer. *Splop!* The tornado spat them out,
scattered them on their backs and dumped
a blanket of leafy grass all over them.

Quick as a flash, Madison picked up
the boys' flashlights, which they'd dropped
in their confusion.

"Oh! I feel sick," Sam moaned, holding his head and spitting out a bit of leaf. He looked pale under his face paint. "What just happened?"

"Who cares? I'm getting out of here!" cried his friend.

"Me too! This place is haunted!" the other yelled.

Madison took pity on them and swung the flashlights around, until she could see the fence. It wasn't very far away at all, and she realized that she must have been running in circles while searching for Storm.

"This way!" The boys weaved about unsteadily as they stumbled toward the exit.

"Wait for me!" Sam bleated in a wobbly voice as he squeezed through the

fence. The sound of retreating footsteps
faded from the street outside.

Laughter bubbled up inside Madison
as she turned back to Storm. He padded
toward her, the last few golden sparks
fading from his fur. "That'll teach them to
mess with us!" she said.

Just then, a tall figure appeared at the gap in the fence.

"Here's Oliver and Ellie now!" Madison guessed, lifting the flashlight. She started to smile, but the grin froze on her face.

Her dad stood there, wearing a furious expression in the flashlight. Madison's heart sank. "I am in *so* much trouble," she whispered.

Storm gave a sympathetic whine. "It is all because of me. I am sorry, Madison."

"It doesn't matter. I'd do the same thing again," she whispered, just before her dad marched forward and stood in front of her with his hands on his hips.

"What were you thinking?" Mr. Berry demanded angrily. "I told you you weren't to come over here by yourself. Why didn't you wait for me?"

"I . . . I had to go after Storm. He ran off . . . because . . . um. He was scared . . . of something . . ." Madison began. She hung her head miserably as she realized that there was no way she could explain how desperate she'd been to find Storm, without giving away his secret.

"I'm sorry, Madison, but that's no excuse," her dad snapped. "You should have called me and we would have looked for Storm together. The way I see it, you ignored what I said, and deliberately ran off without me!"

Madison bit her lip. She knew that he was right. There was nothing she could say in her defense.

Mr. Berry sighed and ran a hand through his hair in exasperation. "Well, you can forget about that night watch! We're going straight back home."

"What? You're grounding me? You can't . . . It's not fair . . ." Madison gasped, but she could see by her dad's face that she was wasting her time.

Mr. Berry turned and marched toward the street, obviously expecting her to follow him. Madison had no choice. She trudged after him, with Storm padding along by her side.

"I don't suppose you've got any magical ideas about how to get me out of this mess, do you?" she whispered hopefully.

Storm shook his head. "I am sorry, Madison. Magic cannot solve everything."

Madison nodded gloomily. "I guess not."

On their way to the house, they saw the Robertsons' jeep pulling up. Madison made a glum face at Ellie and drew one finger across her throat to show that she was in deep trouble with her dad.

Ellie gave her a sympathetic look through the passenger window.

"I hope you find some field mice," Madison called to her. *At least they won't have any trouble from those three boys,* she thought, cheering up a tiny bit as she thought of how Storm had taught them a lesson they wouldn't forget!

Chapter
TEN

Grandma Jen laughed and laughed when Madison told her about the night's events the next morning. Or at least, her own special version of things, with all the magical bits about Storm taken out.

"I wish I'd seen those boys' faces when you threw grass and leaves all over them in the darkness. And the way you made ghost noises to frighten the little beasts, too. That was quick thinking. You're quite a girl, Madison Berry!"

"Um . . . yeah," Madison said looking sideways at Storm as she sprinkled a pinch of fish food into the tank.

Storm was curled up on the recliner next to Grandma Jen. He woofed softly and wagged his tail to show that he didn't mind Madison taking all the credit.

"Anyway, Dad's calmed down now, and I'm allowed to go over to the field with Storm when I get back from visiting you," Madison added. "So I'll be able to find out how Ellie and her dad did last night."

"Oh good," Grandma Jen said. Her face changed as if she had something on her mind. "I'd love to know what happened. Why don't you stop back here this afternoon, and you can tell me all about it."

"Okay, then," Madison said, mildly surprised by her grandma's interest. Usually she was happy to wait until the next time Madison visited for any news.

"Don't forget now," Grandma Jen said, wagging her finger.

Madison found herself wondering if

her grandma might be feeling especially lonely. "Grandma Jen was really set on us going back later, wasn't she?" she commented to Storm as they walked home.

Storm blinked up at her with wise bright blue eyes. "Perhaps she has a special reason."

Madison frowned, wondering what Storm meant. She was about to ask him when they turned onto her street. Storm saw Ellie taking something out of the jeep and bounded toward her.

The older girl spotted him and bent down to stroke him. "Hi, Storm." She stood up and smiled at Madison. "Hi! I'm glad you're here. It's perfect timing. Come with me!"

While they hurried over to where

Oliver was standing in an area of thick
long grass, Ellie explained that they hadn't
had much success with the night watch.
"We only found a few empty nests, like
before. Dad was pretty disappointed,
since it's our last morning here, but then
we noticed that there was some swampy
ground, and we found a clump of nests
hidden in some dense grass. Some nests
were even built in old box traps that must
have been left here a long time ago!"

Oliver looked across at the girls.
"Don't come any closer," he warned.
"Your shoes will get stuck in the wet
mud!" He pulled a long plank of wood
across the swampy ground. "You can stand
on this and peek in, if you're careful."

Madison's pulse quickened with
anticipation as she cautiously stepped on

the piece of wood. Lifting the lid of the box trap, she peered inside. She could see a cozy woven nest and inside, curled up and fast asleep, were three baby field mice. The first she had ever seen!

Her eyes widened with wonder as she took in their rounded bodies, long tails, and dainty little pink paws. Their fur was more gray than dark brown, and they had long white whiskers.

After a few moments, she silently closed the lid and stepped back.

Storm stood waiting for her, wagging his tail. Madison bent down to stroke him. "Sorry I can't show them to you," she whispered. "But I don't think Oliver would let me take you into the swamp!"

Storm shrugged his furry little shoulders. "I do not mind. After all, I cannot chase them like rabbits!" he woofed playfully.

Madison grinned at her little friend and then turned back to Oliver. "How old are those babies, and how come the mother field mice are using the boxes?"

"About a week old. The babies will be ready to leave in a little while," Oliver told her. "The mothers obviously feel safer in the boxes, because they don't get disturbed by people walking dogs and kids building hideouts and stuff."

"So it's official!" Madison said. "This field's had a furry secret all this time, and we didn't know it!"

Oliver laughed. "That's one way of putting it. I've been in contact with the local wildlife trust, and there's talk of making the field into a nature preserve."

"Wow! That's fantastic!" Madison said. "I saw a TV show about nature preserves. They need lots of volunteers to help make paths and dig ponds and stuff."

"Really?" Oliver said, his eyes

twinkling. "Do you know anyone who might be interested?"

"Definitely!" Madison said, beaming back at him.

After making plans to keep in touch with Ellie and Oliver, Madison took Storm for a good long walk and then stopped home to tell her mom the amazing news before setting out for Grandma Jen's as promised.

Storm ran along beside her as they turned onto her grandmother's street. They were just passing a small play area surrounded by bushes when Storm gave a whine of terror and shot toward the slide and swings.

Instantly alert this time, Madison heard a faint growling and snapping noise. She whipped around to see dark shapes looking into the front yard a few houses away. Sunlight glinted on their pale eyes and extra-sharp teeth.

She gasped. Shadow's dogs! Storm was in terrible danger. The moment she had been dreading was here. Her heart pounded as she dashed into the little playground just as a bright flash of gold lit up the bushes behind the swings. Madison rushed forward and pushed through the branches.

Storm stood there, a tiny black-tan-and-white puppy no longer, but a majestic young silver-gray wolf with a glittering neck ruff. An older she-wolf with a gentle face stood next to him.

Tears pricked Madison's eyes. "Your enemies are here! Save yourself, Storm!" she burst out.

Storm's big midnight-blue eyes
glowed with affection. "You have been a
good friend, Madison. Be of good heart,"
he said in a velvety growl.

"I'll never forget you, Storm,"
Madison said, her voice catching.

There was a final dazzling flash and
a silent explosion of large gold sparks
that sprinkled around Madison like
fairy dust and crackled as they went out.

Storm and his mother faded and then were gone.

A furious snarling sounded at the entrance to the play area, and then all was silent.

Madison stood there, stunned by how fast it had all happened. Her heart ached, but she was glad that she'd had a chance to say good-bye to her magical friend. She knew that she would always remember the adventure she had shared with him.

As Madison walked out of the play area, she looked up with tears in her eyes to see Grandma Jen standing at her gate, holding onto her walker. A young woman stood next to her, holding a tiny black-tan-and-white beagle puppy. There was a van with an ANIMAL RESCUE sign on the side parked nearby.

"Madison! I've got a surprise for you! Come and meet my new puppy. I've enjoyed having Storm around so much that I couldn't resist. Especially as my expert granddaughter has promised to help me look after him!"

He even looks a bit like Storm, Madison thought delightedly. So this was why her grandmother had insisted that she come back for a second visit.

"Here you are." The woman handed her the warm furry bundle. "Your grandma says you can give him a name."

Madison smiled down at the new puppy as he gave a scared little whine. There could never be another Storm, but she knew exactly what she was going to call this new friend.

"Hello, Magic," she crooned, looking
down into the puppy's melting brown
eyes. "You and I are going to get along
really well!"

About the Author

Sue Bentley's books for children often include animals or fairies. She lives in Northampton, England, and enjoys reading, going to the movies, and sitting watching the frogs and newts in her garden pond. If she hadn't been a writer, she would probably have been a skydiver or brain surgeon. The main reason she writes is that she can drink pots and pots of tea while she's typing. She has met and owned many cats and dogs, and each one has brought a special sort of magic to her life.

Don't miss these Magic Ponies books!

Don't miss these Magic Kitten books!

#1 A Summer Spell

#2 Classroom Chaos

#3 Star Dreams

#4 Double Trouble

#5 Moonlight Mischief

#6 A Circus Wish

#7 Sparkling Steps

#8 A Glittering Gallop

#9 Seaside Mystery

#10 Firelight Friends

#11 A Shimmering Splash

#12 A Puzzle of Paws

#13 Picture Perfect

#14 A Splash of Forever

A Christmas Surprise

Purrfect Sticker
and Activity Book

Starry Sticker
and Activity Book

Don't miss these Magic Puppy books!

Don't miss these Magic Bunny books!

#1 Chocolate Wishes

#2 Vacation Dreams

#3 A Splash of Magic

#4 Classroom Capers

#5 Dancing Days